OLIVER

BY

Pioneer Valley Educational Press, Inc.

Here is Oliver.
Oliver is hungry.
He is looking
for some food.
"Meow!" said Oliver.

3

Here is Oliver's bowl.
"Meow!" said Oliver.

"Meow! Meow! Meow!"
said Oliver.
Oliver is hungry!
Oliver is looking
for some food.

"Evan!" said Mom.
"Come here
and feed Oliver.
Oliver is hungry!"

"Look, Oliver,"
said Evan.
"Here is some food
for you."

Oliver is a happy cat.
"Purr," said Oliver.
"Purr! Purr!"